THE MYSTERIOUS WORLD OF COSENTINO

Job C

For those who believe in magic.
—COS

For Adam Keighley, who once showed me an amazing
magic trick—and, after much begging, showed me how to do it
—Jack Heath

For my Nans and my kids' Nans. Nanas are the best
—James Hart

First American Edition 2018
Kane Miller,
A Division of EDC Publishing
PO Box 470663
Tulsa, OK 74147-0663

Text & illustrations copyright © Scholastic Australia, 2017.
Text by Cosentino with Jack Heath.
Illustrations by James Hart.

Internal images: p27 and various pages, Stars © Alisovna/Creative MarketFirst

First published by Scholastic Australia division of Scholastic Australia Pty Limited in 2018
This edition published under license from Scholastic Australia Pty Limited

www.kanemiller.com
www.edcpub.com
www.usbornebooksandmore.com

Library of Congress Control Number: 2017958890

Printed and bound in the United States of America

1 2 3 4 5 6 7 8 9 10

ISBN: 978-1-61067-750-9

RABBIT RESCUE

By

THE GRAND ILLUSIONIST

WITH JACK HEATH
ILLUSTRATED BY JAMES HART

Kane Miller
A DIVISION OF EDC PUBLISHING

THE MYSTERIOUS WORLD OF COSENTINO

COPPERTOWN

COSENTINO

Magician at Copperpot Theater
Abilities: Escape, Sleight of hand, telekinesis, Illusion

LOCKI

Cos's partner at Copperpot Theater
Abilities: Lock picking

SNUGGLES

Lettuce disposal expert in Cos's hat
Abilities: Appearing and disappearing, heightened senses

PROFESSOR CAMOUFLAGE

Celebrity Impersonator at Siegfried Alley
(since escaping from the Royal Zoo)
Abilities: Can disguise himself as anything

NONNA

Prop/costume designer
Copperfield Cottage
Abilities: Healing powers

ACE

Former soldier in the Army of 52
Abilities: Transformation

THE MYSTERIOUS WORLD OF COSENTINO

SiLVER CaSTLE, SiLVER CiTY

HOLLOW

King's henchman
Abilities: Can smell magic

THE KiNG OF DiaMONDS

King of Magicland
Abilities: Hypnotism

FLEX

King's bodyguard
Abilities: Superstrong

PRINCESS PRiSCiLLA

Princess of Magicland
Abilities: Levitation, sweet, kind heart,
extremely clever

MatchMan

King's henchman
Abilities: Fire powers

CHaNCE

King's dog
Abilities: Lucky

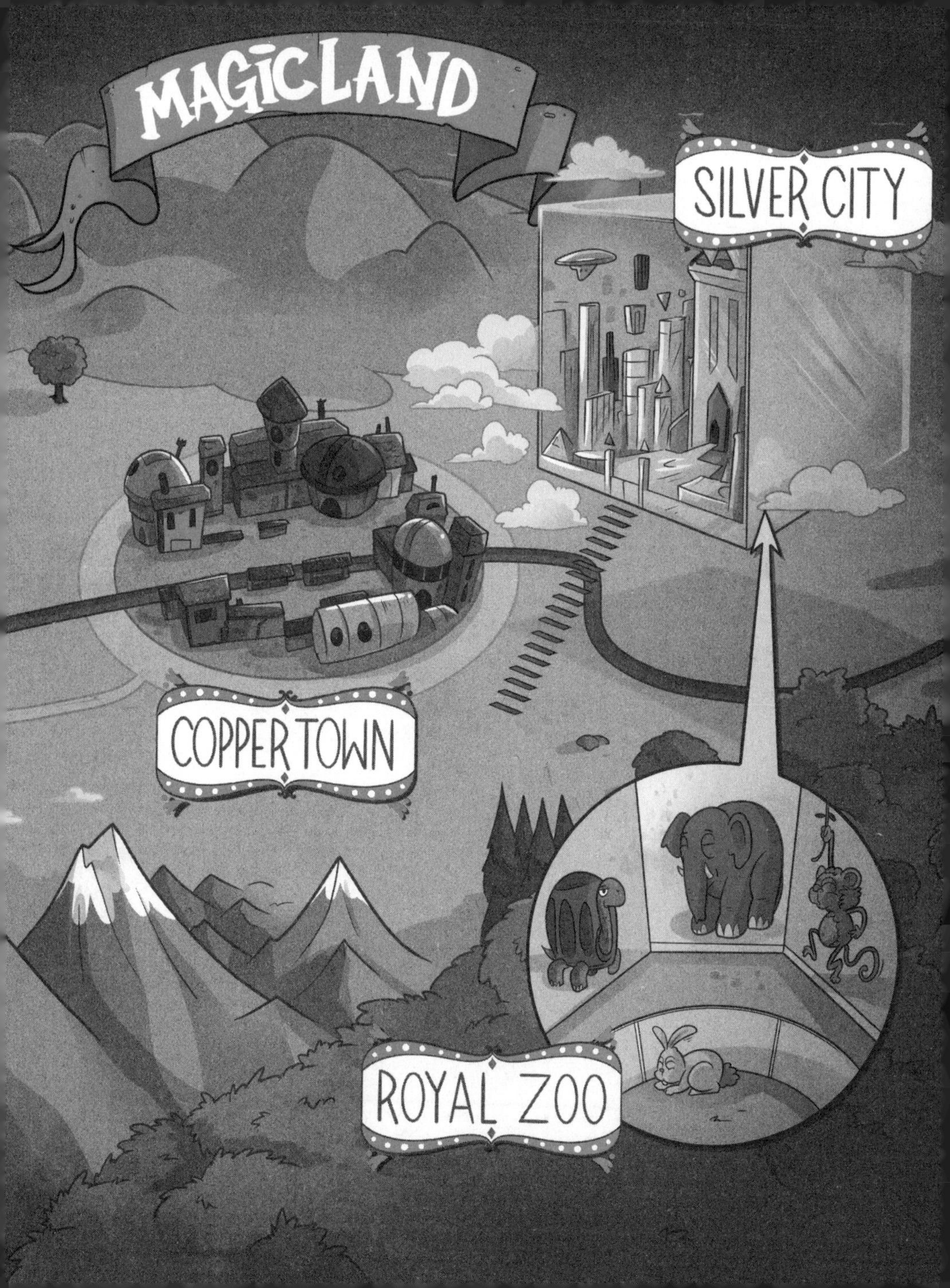
MAGIC LAND
SILVER CITY
COPPER TOWN
ROYAL ZOO

SHISH KEBAB

Cos **revved** the chain saw. **VVVRUMMM.**

The volunteer looked **terrified**. Her middle was hidden inside a wooden box, but both ends of her had turned totally green!

"Keep your peel on," Cos said. "This won't hurt a bit." He turned to the huge crowd crammed into the Copperpot Theater. They stared at the chain saw in terrified silence. "OK," Cos said, "let's make a **banana smoothie!**"

"What?" the banana yelped.

Cos chuckled. "Oh, silly me.

I MEANT
TO SAY

BANANA
SPLIT!"

He lowered the chain saw to the box.

Cos pushed the box apart, revealing the two halves of the banana. Everyone cheered.

Cos put the chain saw aside and put the box back together. The crowd whooped and cheered as he helped the shaky banana back to her seat.

The show was going well. After Cos and his friends' recent escape from the King, Hollow and his Army of 52, everyone in Coppertown wanted to see his magic. Cos had been worried that the King and his men would keep searching for him and the other prisoners who escaped The Arcade, but no one had shown up yet. So it was back to business as usual. So far that night, Cos had done some card tricks and some rope tricks. Snuggles had used her **disappearing powers** to steal the keys from an audience member's pocket, and Cos had made them **reappear** inside a block of ice (who was very surprised).

There were just two tricks to go.

"For my next illusion," Cos said, "I'm going to need another **volunteer**."

He lowered his hat, shielding his eyes from the stage lights. He scanned the crowd.

No hands were raised. In fact, some wide-eyed people had folded their arms, or sat on them, as if they were worried their hands might escape into the air.

"This trick is completely safe," Cos promised. "Well, fairly safe. For the volunteer, anyway."

Still there was silence. Everyone was too scared to come up.

Cos pointed at a wooden man with a bright-orange head. "What's your name, sir?"

The wooden man looked around, as though hoping Cos was talking to someone else.

"Yes, you," Cos said. "The redhead. What's your name?"

MATCHMAN

AN ANGRY MATCH
ABILITIES: FIRE POWERS

"I'm Matchman," the wooden man mumbled.

"I'm sorry?" Cos said.

"Matchman!" the man repeated.

"I heard you, I'm just sorry." Cos grinned and winked at the crowd. "Come on up, Matchman. Let's give him a hand, ladies and gentlemen!"

The crowd applauded as Matchman
reluctantly joined Cos up on the stage.

"Can you hear me OK?" Cos asked.

"Fine," Matchman said.

"ARE YOU SURE? THERE'S SOMETHING IN YOUR EAR."

"I don't have ears," Matchman said.

Ignoring him, Cos reached out and pulled a small orange ball from the side of Matchman's head. He put it in his pocket.

"That wasn't in my ear," Matchman **growled**.

"I can't hear you." Cos pulled a second orange ball out of his own ear. The audience laughed.

"Stop it!" Matchman snarled.

"You don't like this trick?" Cos looked disappointed. "OK. I'll make the ball **vanish**."

He clenched the ball in his fist. He squeezed tighter and tighter, grimacing.

Then he opened his fist, and FOUR balls jumped out of it!

The crowd applauded.

"Enough!" Matchman yelled.

"OK, OK. Nonna!"

A fierce-looking old lady walked out of the wings, dragging a giant sword and a watermelon.

This is Nonna! She makes the props for my shows!

"But I was too busy to make a prop sword," Nonna said. "So I just found a real one."

She threw the watermelon into the air.

She sliced it in half with the giant sword.

Swish!

"You were supposed to make a **trick** sword!" Cos said.

Nonna held a hand up to her ear. "I'm sorry?"

"A trick sword!" Cos repeated.

"I heard you, I'm just sorry." Grinning, Nonna handed the sword to Cos and walked off the stage.

"OK," Cos said shakily.

NONNA

PROP/COSTUME DESIGNER
COPPERFIELD COTTAGE,
COPPERTOWN
ABILITIES: HEALING POWERS

"THIS TRICK IS GOING TO BE MORE **DANGEROUS** THAN I **EXPECTED.**"

Cos held the tip of
the blade against his
chest, and then passed
the handle to Matchman.

"All you need to do," Cos
said, "is stab me through the
heart."

A gasp arose from the crowd.
Matchman's eyes widened.

"On the count of three," Cos told
him, "I want you to push as hard as
you can. One—"

Matchman didn't wait for three. He
pushed the handle so hard that Cos's hat
fell off.

The sword plunged through Cos's chest.

BURNING DOWN THE HOUSE

Someone **screamed** as the sword popped out of Cos's back. The tip skewered his falling hat.

Cos staggered backward, pulling the handle out of Matchman's grasp. He looked down at the blade sticking out of his chest.

IS THERE a DOCTOR iN THE HOUSE?

GASP!

There was horrified silence from the audience.

But Cos knew something they didn't. Nonna had made him a trick sword.

MAGIC SECRET UNLOCKED

The blade wasn't really through his heart—it had slid back into the handle, like a telescope. A steel plate was strapped to Cos's chest, so when Matchman had tried to push the sword through it, the blade had retracted instead. The plate was uncomfortable, but Cos had been wearing it every day for weeks, learning to move naturally with it underneath his clothes.
A second blade was fixed to Cos's back.

The second-hardest part of the trick was making sure the second blade popped out at exactly the right moment, so it looked like part of the original sword. The hardest part was this . . .

Cos turned to face
the audience, hiding his
back. Then he pulled the
sword out of his chest
and **tossed** it into the
air. He threw it high, so
the audience's eyes were
well away from him.

While everyone was looking at the flying sword, Cos reached behind his back and folded the second blade away, under his T-shirt. Then he reached up and caught the falling sword.

He raised his shirt, lifting the steel plate at the same time, showing his bare skin to the audience. His chest was intact.

Cheers and claps erupted from the audience. People whistled and stomped their feet.

Cos had expected Matchman to be delighted by the trick, or at least relieved that Cos wasn't hurt. But instead, Matchman looked angry. His orange scalp glowed with quiet fury. Some people didn't like feeling tricked, Cos knew. But those people didn't usually come to magic shows.

"You can go back to your seat now," Cos told him.

Woohoo!

Matchman bowed like a Samurai warrior, and climbed down the stairs off the stage. Cos saw a logo stamped on the back of Matchman's head. It was a picture of a seal. The symbol seemed familiar, but Cos wasn't sure where he had seen it before.

Instead of returning to his seat, Matchman walked up the aisle and out through the exit.

YAY!

Cos forced a smile. "That was an illusion," he told the crowd.

"BUT THiS NeXT PART OF THe PeRFORMaNCe iS VeRY ReaL."

He walked to the rear of the stage and pulled back a curtain, revealing a steel box.

This is a hypobaric chamber!

"Once I'm inside, the door will be locked and all the oxygen will be sucked out by this pump. I can hold my breath for about two minutes. Hopefully that will be long enough to pick the lock and get the door open . . ."

Cos paused. He could smell smoke. But he hadn't performed any fire tricks tonight.

There was a strange flickering glow near the exit, behind the audience.

Cos realized two things at the same time.

ONE: THE SYMBOL ON THE BACK OF MATCHMAN'S HEAD HAD BEEN THE KING'S ROYAL SEAL.

TWO: THE THEATER WAS ON FIRE!

SHOWSTOPPERS

The back row of audience members noticed the crackling flames a split second after Cos did.

"Fire!" someone shrieked.

People started scrambling out of their seats. But there was only one exit, and it was burning. Matchman had probably blocked it from outside.

There was no way out.

"Get up on the stage!" Cos yelled, beckoning. "Come on! Up here!"

The audience ran away from the growing flames toward the stage. The back rows of seats were already burning. Cos figured he had a minute at the most before the fire reached the stage.

What do we do?

We're going out the back way!

There is no back way!

Not yet!

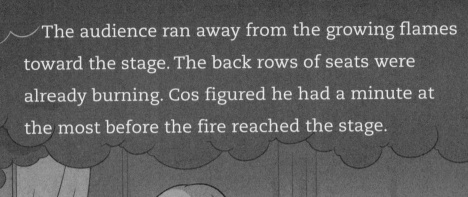

Cos ran over to the wings. Two chain saws sat side by side on a shelf.

MAGIC SECRET UNLOCKED

One was real—he had used it to cut through a thick log earlier in the show. The other was fake. He had made the switch behind the fallen log, so he could pretend to run the fake blade through the box with the banana in it.

Cos grabbed the real chain saw and pulled the starter cord. The motor started with a deafening **snarl**.

He carried the chain saw through the crowd toward the back of the stage. The fire had eaten five rows of seats, and was getting closer to the front. He was **running out of time**.

As Cos cut through the rear wall of the stage he could hardly see through the smoke. The handle of the chain saw was hot. Sweat dribbled into his eyes. He could hear screaming. It sounded like the fire had almost reached the stage.

Cos had cut a rectangle into the wall. Cool air from outside streamed through the cuts.

Cos gave the wall a mighty kick. The rectangle popped out, showering splinters.

Cos stepped aside, ushering the crowd through the gap into the alley behind the theater. "Go, go!"

The crowd ran through. The banana slipped, but Nonna helped her up. Locki was last through the hole.

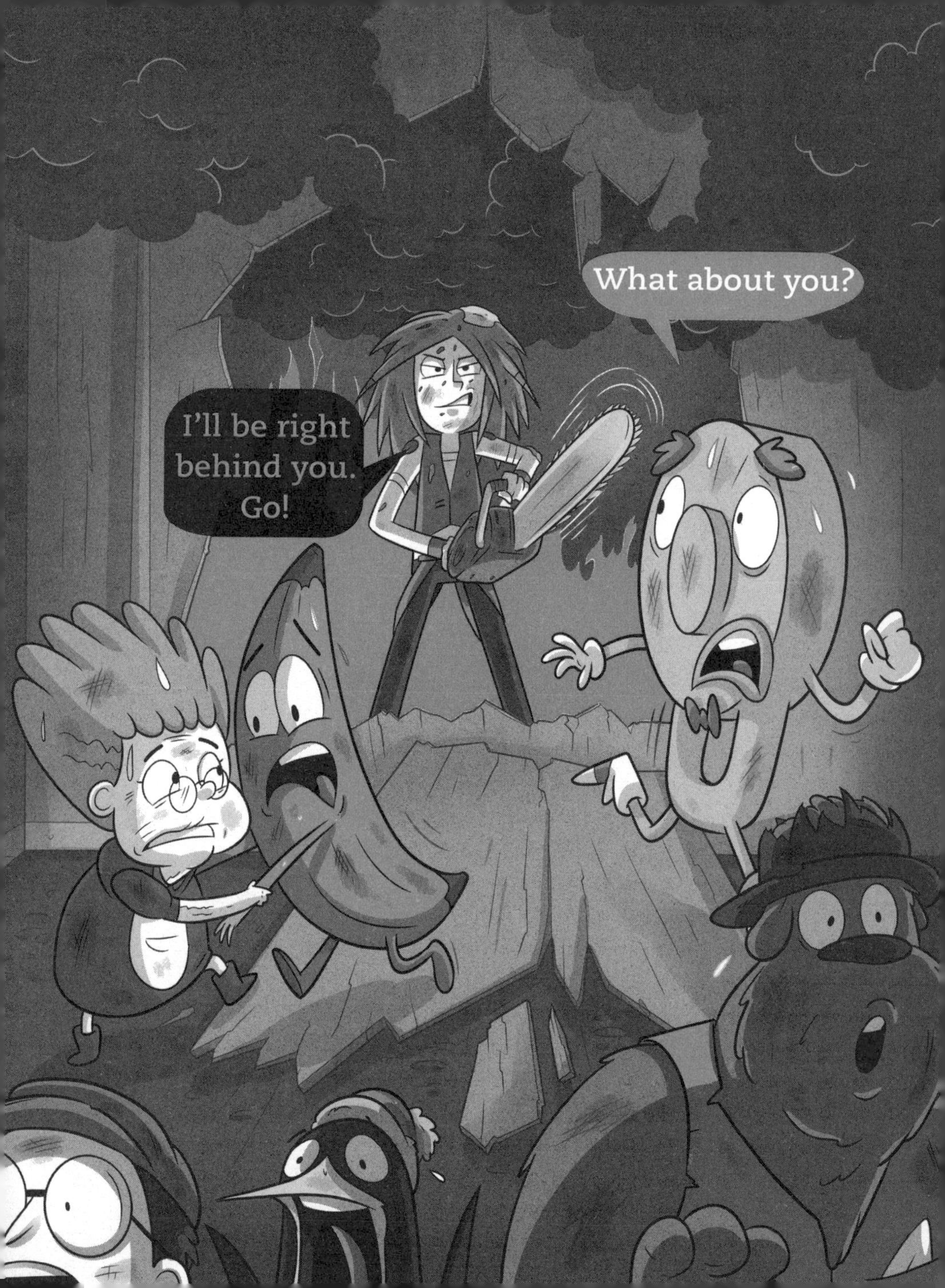
What about you?
I'll be right behind you. Go!

Cos couldn't leave the theater until he was
sure everyone else had made it out.

Cos turned and ran back **toward the fire**. He
jumped off the stage into the aisle, where the
flames burned higher and higher, **popping** and
spitting.

Hello? Is anybody
still in here?

Cos took a deep breath and crouched down to look under the seats. The smoke **stung** his eyes. It was just as deadly as the fire—if he breathed it in it would **poison** him.

He had lied to the audience. He could actually hold his breath for three minutes and thirty-nine seconds. That was how long he had to make it out of here.

He peered down the aisles.

No one.

He climbed back onto the stage and checked in the wings.

No one.

With about two minutes of air left in his lungs, he decided that he'd done all he could. It was time to leave.

Cos grabbed the rigging and tried to drag it out of the way. But it was too **heavy**. It usually took three stagehands to move it. And the flames were getting closer.

His heart pounding, Cos backed away from the fire. He only had about **THIRTY SECONDS OF AIR LEFT**. His chest **ached**.

There must be a way out of this. He was a magician. He had **cheated death** hundreds of times in his daring escapes—

Escapes. The hypobaric chamber!

Cos ran over to the steel box. He grabbed the handle and **heaved** the door open.

The flames were right behind Cos now. The heat was unbearable. He was running out of air.

Going inside the chamber wouldn't help. The flames would cook the box and he would be

46

roasted alive. But the fire could only keep burning if there was oxygen in the air.

Cos switched on the air pump.

The pump made a WHIRRING noise. It was only supposed to suck the oxygen out of the hypobaric chamber—but because the door was open, it sucked all the oxygen out of the theater!

WHIR

Help me!

The fire flickered and died. The theater was safe—but Cos couldn't breathe. Just like the fire, he needed oxygen.

"Help me!" he gasped. But no one heard him, and he slipped down, down, down into the darkness of sleep.

RABBIT TRAP

The King of Diamonds glared at Jennie the elephant. Jennie glared back at him.

They were in the grounds of the royal zoo. The elephant sat on a pile of straw behind a pane of glass. The glass was thin, but the King had cast a **spell** on it. It wouldn't break, no matter how hard the elephant charged. The padlock sealing the window shut was only unlocked once a day so food could be thrown into the enclosure.

Having two heads was a pain in the neck. It was never clear who was in charge.

"The elephant won't do a handstand," the other head continued. "She's not **evil** enough."

The King had the power of **mind control**. He could make anyone do anything, *if* they had a drop of evil in their heart, which almost everyone did.

But not this elephant, apparently. She was so kind and brave that the King couldn't make her do even the simplest tricks.

"Let's go see the monkeys," the other head suggested. "They're always **naughty**. Easy to control."

"Very well," the King grumbled. With a last grim glance at the elephant—who looked smug—he plodded toward the monkey house.

On his way, he passed the rabbit cages. Hundreds of rabbits were trapped behind the glass, sipping water from upturned bottles.

"Have they got enough food?" he asked.

"Looks like it," his other head said.

The King tapped one of the enclosures and said, "Good."

The King was about to **yell** at the rude rabbit when a young woman appeared farther up the path, escorted by Flex, the King's bodyguard.

Princess Priscilla was the King's niece. Like Jennie the elephant, she had no evil in her heart and couldn't be controlled. But unlike the elephant, the King couldn't trap her in a glass cage. People would ask questions.

Priscilla, where have you been?

You sent for me, your majesty?

Both the King's heads nodded. "I did. I need you to make some invitations to my birthday party. Send them magically—that'll impress the guests. Invite all the lords, ladies, duchesses, dukes, counts, countesses, baronesses and barons."

But not the earls.

Earls are shifty.

"Of course, your majesty," Priscilla said, and she used her **levitation ability** to hold a pen in mid-air while it wrote on magical paper containing the royal seal. "What are the details?"

"The party will be held at the royal palace tomorrow night," the King said. "Six o'clock sharp."

He looked out over the thousands of rabbits.

"Tell them dinner will be . . .

ROLLED ROAST RABBIT!"

THE COTTAGE

Cos was lying on a soft brown couch. Sunlight streamed through the lacy curtains. A big clock ticked quietly on the mantle.

"No," Cos mumbled, still half-asleep. "It can't be appendicitis. My ankle hurts!"

"You're awake!" someone said.

Cos sat up. His skin was **tender** from the heat of the fire, and some of his hair had burned away. But he was **alive**. How?

The clock **squirmed** and **shivered**. With a loud **POP**, it turned into a lizard.

"Professor Camouflage!" Cos said. "Where am I?"

"Don't you recognize it?" the Professor asked. "It's Nonna's cottage. I'll tell her you're awake."

The Professor transformed into a bird and flapped out the window into the backyard.

Cos looked around. Yes, this was Nonna's cottage. He felt a stab of guilt—he hadn't been here since he was a little boy, even though Nonna came to his theater all the time.

His theater! He hoped it was OK. It wasn't just where he put on his shows—it was his home. He even slept in the attic, on a camping mattress. His illegal spell book was hidden there too.

Nonna entered the room, with Ace and Locki.

Nonna released him.

"How are you feeling, Cos?" Ace asked.

"Crispy," Cos said. "But alive. Did everyone else make it out OK?"

Nonna nodded. "Ace dug through the wreckage, and Locki shut down the oxygen pump."

Of course, Cos thought. Locki was a padlock, so he didn't need to breathe. And Ace was a spade—Cos should have guessed he'd be good at digging.

Nonna put a cup of **bubbling** purple liquid on the table. It smelled **foul**, but when Cos sipped it, his skin stopped hurting and his hair started to grow back. It was one of Nonna's **healing potions**.

"The theater," he said. "Is it . . ."

Locki shook his head sadly. "It's pretty wrecked, Cos. The building is still standing, and the fire didn't reach the attic—so I found your spell book—but the seats burned up, along with all the costumes and the props."

Cos put his face in his hands, imagining the **damage**. "My props! The shadow box, the zombie ball, the linking rings . . . we can't perform without them."

THE ZOMBIE BALL

THE SHADOW BOX

THE LINKING RINGS

"Was it our fault?" Nonna said. "Did our dead-drop rope catch fire too early?"

Cos shook his head. "We didn't start the fire."

"No, we didn't light it," Locki added. "We tried to fight it."

"Matchman had the royal seal on the back of his head," Cos said.

"I THiNK THE KiNG SENT HiM TO KiLL Me."

"This is my fault," Ace said. "If you hadn't helped me hide from the King, he wouldn't even know who you were."

It's not your fault. I thought the King would forget all about us.

Because the evil King had two heads, he was easily confused and forgetful. Each head always expected the other to remember things.

Professor Camouflage patted Cos's shoulder with a scaly claw. "There's an abandoned theater on Teller Street," he said. "The Incredible Wanda used to perform there. The King was going to demolish it, but we could fix it up. Some new curtains and a coat of paint might do it."

Wanda Magellan was a master magician from long ago. Cos had never met her, but she was the author of his spell book, and her picture had been on Nonna's wall for as long as he could remember. Wanda had disappeared years ago, and everyone assumed the King's troops had caught her practicing illegal magic.

"But we still wouldn't have props, or the money to make them," Cos said. "Even if we fixed up Wanda's theater, I don't know how we'd stop the King from demolishing it anyway."

"Snuggles!" Cos said. "I forgot about you."

"I noticed that," Snuggles said. "Right around the time

a GiaNT SWORD PUNCHED THROUGH MY HoMe!"

Snuggles lived in Cos's hat. She had first appeared in there during a stage show, **startling** Cos and the audience. Fortunately, they thought it was part of his act. She was excellent at hiding—sometimes even Cos couldn't tell if she was in the hat or not. He wasn't surprised she had managed to evade the sword.

"Sorry, Snuggles," Cos said. "That wasn't supposed to happen. We'll get you a new hat to live in."

"Do it fast," Snuggles said. "The hole is letting drafts in."

Cos was about to reply when a puff of spelldust exploded out of his pocket.

Everyone **jumped**.

"No spells in my house!" Nonna said sternly. "I don't want Hollow sniffing around."

"That wasn't me," Cos said. He pulled a folded piece of paper out of his pocket. A trickle of **spelldust** fell out with it.

"What's that?" Locki asked.

"I have no idea." Cos turned the piece of paper over. The King's royal seal was stamped on the back.

Everyone stared at it in silence.

"Maybe it's an apology," Ace said finally. "For burning the theater."

"I doubt it," Cos said. He unfolded the note and showed it to the others.

The rabbits are in trouble! Meet me at the Land of Lost Hats. ~P

"Who is 'P'?" asked Nonna.

"Someone with the power to **teleport** objects," Cos said. "And with access to royal notepaper."

"It must be a trap," Locki said.

Cos shook his head. "If the King knew where we were, he wouldn't send a magic note to my pocket. He'd send his soldiers."

"Why the Land of Lost Hats?" Ace asked. "I thought all the rabbits lived in the island of Warren."

Snuggles sniffed, and pulled out a rumpled piece of newspaper that had clearly been folded and unfolded many times. Everyone looked at the picture.

"All the rabbits in Magicland once used magic hats to teleport back and forth between Coppertown and Warren, a web of tunnels beyond the sea," she said. "When the King banned magic in Coppertown, all the magic hats were turned into regular hats and dumped at the edge of town. This article says most of the rabbits stayed in Warren, but a few, like me, were stranded in Coppertown forever."

MAGIC HATS BANNED!

The King has outlawed the use of all magic hats. Rabbits have been relocated to Warren, permanently.

Rabbits safe in Warren

Cos patted Snuggles on the head. Talking about Warren or the Land of Lost Hats always made Snuggles sad.

"I vote we go check it out," Cos said. "Who's with me?"

"I'll go," said Professor Camouflage. "If it's a **trap**, you'll need backup."

"I'll come too," said Snuggles. "We can get a new hat."

"Good idea," Cos said. "Bring your spare ears, so we can make sure they attach properly."

Snuggles owned a fake pair of ears which she sometimes stuck to the inside of Cos's hat. They made it look like she was hiding in the hat when she wasn't, which was useful for disappearing tricks. It also stopped other rabbits from stealing the hat.

"The King's soldiers patrol the Land of Lost Hats," Ace warned. "Coppertown residents aren't allowed there."

"Why not?" Cos asked.

Ace shrugged. "Who knows why the King does anything?"

"Snuggles can disappear and the Professor can transform himself," Nonna said, "but Cos will need a disguise. I'll get my sewing kit."

As the others bustled around, Cos stared at the note. Who, or what, was P? And what kind of trouble could the rabbits be in?

THE LAND OF LOST HATS

The Land of Lost Hats appeared on the horizon soon after they left Coppertown. At first it was just a black smudge in the distance, but as they got closer, the place took shape.

Towers of hats **teetered** atop mountains of hats. Rivers of hats flowed down into lakes of hats. Black silk ribbons shone from between velvet brims. There were **top hats, fedoras, BOWLER HATS, PORKPIE HATS, baseball caps** . . .

Nonna had whipped up a **perfect disguise** for Cos. He wore two big sheets of cardboard on his front and back, painted to make him look like a playing card—the Six of Hearts, part of the King's Army of 52. Coppertown residents weren't allowed in the Land of Lost Hats, but the King's soldiers could go wherever they liked.

As Cos trudged onto the dark landscape, he wondered what he was standing on. It didn't seem like there was solid ground beneath the hats—just more hats. He felt like he might get sucked down into the black mass at any moment.

The Professor was counting hats. "Seven million, six hundred and fifty-four thousand, three hundred and twenty-one hats," he said. "Seven million, six hundred and fifty-four thousand, three hundred and twenty-two hats.

Seven million, six hundred and—"

"See any you like, Snuggles?" Cos asked.

"No." Snuggles pawed **morosely** at one of the ribbons.

"Well, don't worry," Cos said. "By the Professor's count there are seven million, six hundred and fifty-four thousand, three hundred and twenty-two other hats to choose from. We'll find you something."

"Any sign of the **mysterious P**?" the Professor asked. He spun a hat on his claw and tossed it onto his head.

"No," Cos said. "Maybe—"

Then he spotted someone in the distance. A young woman. She was dressed as a Coppertowner, but her clothes were too clean, and had no tears.

"Is that . . ." Snuggles began.

Cos nodded. "Princess Priscilla. The King's niece.

What's she doing here?"

Priscilla spotted them and ran over. "You got my note," she said. "Sorry to make you meet me all the way out here. I didn't want to risk being seen."

Cos didn't know whether to **trust** Priscilla. She had once convinced the King not to behead Cos, and she had also provided a distraction so Cos could escape from prison. But Cos didn't know if she had saved his life out of **kindness**, or if she was just using him. She was from Silver City, a floating world of rich people who **hated** Coppertown.

"I don't know what you're talking about," he said.

The Professor nudged him. "Don't you see, Cos? She's the one who sent the message."

"What message?" Cos said, winking furiously at the Professor. "I am Six of Hearts, loyal soldier to the King."

"The message which magically appeared in your pocket," the Professor said.

Cos sighed.

"For magicians," Priscilla said, "your friends are surprisingly bad at trickery."

"You said the rabbits are in trouble," Snuggles said. "Is the King going to attack Warren?"

"The rabbits aren't in Warren," Priscilla said. "The King captured them all before he disenchanted the hats. Then he let everyone think the rabbits were in Warren. They're actually prisoners in the royal zoo."

"THE ZOO?" Professor Camouflage cried. "I was trapped in the King's zoo for many years. It's horrible!"

"You didn't see any rabbits while you were there?" Cos asked.

"I hardly saw anything while I was there," the Professor said. "The residents are kept separate. It's **VERY, VERY, VERY BORING**. That's how I got so good at counting."

"Trust me, the rabbits are there," Priscilla said. "That's why Coppertown people aren't allowed in the Land of Lost Hats. The King is afraid someone will re-enchant one of the hats and use it to travel to Warren. Then they'll realize the rabbits aren't there."

"Cos," Snuggles said. "We have to get them out of there."

"I want to help the rabbits escape, too," Priscilla told Cos. "I thought you, being an escape artist, could help."

"We're in," Snuggles said immediately. "I'm Snuggles, by the way."

"I haven't finished," Priscilla said. "We have to break them out by tomorrow night.

THE KING IS PLANNING TO HAVE THE RABBITS FOR HIS BIRTHDAY DINNER!"

"Dinner at the royal palace?" the Professor said.

Everyone stared at him.

"Ohhhhh," the Professor said. "He's going to eat them. Right. Gotcha."

Cos said, "So let's see if I have this right . . .

"ONE: REMEMBER, WE'RE ALREADY WANTED FUGITIVES,

TWO: YOU NEED US TO BREAK INTO THE KING'S PALACE,

THREE: SECURITY IS EXTRA TIGHT, SINCE IT'S HIS BIRTHDAY,

FOUR: YOU WANT US TO HELP HUNDREDS OF RABBITS ESCAPE, AND

FIVE: ALL THIS HAS TO HAPPEN WITHIN THE NEXT TWENTY-FOUR HOURS?"

"Pretty much," Priscilla said. "But—"

"Cos!" Snuggles pointed to the top of a nearby hill. "Look!"

Cos squinted up at the hill. "What's that?"

"It's a dog," Snuggles said. "Sort of."

"Sort of?"

"It's square."

Cos looked again at the top of the hill and sure enough, there it was, a dog, wagging its tail and sniffing the hats beneath its paws.

"The name on her collar is 'Chance,'" said Snuggles, who had amazing eyesight.

Priscilla paled. "That's the King's dog!" she hissed.

Cos was starting to feel nervous. What was the King's dog doing up here?

"She won't be alone," he said. "Can you see anything else, Snuggles?"

"No," Snuggles said. "But I can hear people coming."

Now Cos could hear them too. It was the sound of boots **crushing** hats, coming up the hill behind the dog. The King's Army of 52 was here. Maybe not all of them, but enough to cause trouble.

Priscilla pointed to Cos's costume. "Is that thing solid?"

Cos tapped the cardboard.

Solid enough. Why?

I have a plan . . .

Dogs Chasing Rabbits

Hollow was panting by the time he had climbed the hill. Two soldiers were waiting for him at the top. Chance, the King's dog, was chasing her tail excitedly.

Chance was the world's luckiest dog. Hollow often took her with him when

CHANCE

KING'S DOG
SILVER CASTLE, SILVER CITY
ABILITIES: LUCKY

he was **hunting** lawbreakers. Other dogs could sometimes sniff out fugitives, but Chance always seemed to stumble across them just by luck.

"Do you still have Priscilla in your sights?" Hollow asked. When he saw her leaving Silver City, he'd asked the soldiers to follow her. He had a **hunch** that she couldn't be trusted.

"Yes, sir," said one of the soldiers, the Three of Diamonds. "She's down there, talking to a lizard, a rabbit and a soldier."

"Which soldier?" Hollow asked.

"The Six of Hearts, sir."

"Hey," said the other soldier. "I'm the Six of Hearts!"

Hollow and Three looked at him. It was true. Chance wagged her tail.

Hollow raised a pair of jewel-encrusted binoculars.

The dog was right. That wasn't a soldier at all. It was Cosentino, the Grand Illusionist!

"I might have known," Hollow growled. "On the count of three, I want you to run down and grab them."

Six of Hearts looked uncertain. "Even the Princess, my lord?"

Hollow hesitated. "No. Just the others."

The group below didn't seem to know they were being watched. Cosentino was trying on hats, frowning as he adjusted and then discarded each one.

"ONE," Hollow whispered.

"TWO—"

97

And then Cosentino suddenly threw one of the
hats straight up into the air.

It landed right next to Cosentino—but his three accomplices had vanished completely.

Hollow choked on his own spit.

"WHAT?! GET DOWN THERE!"

he roared.

"GO, GO, GO!"

The two soldiers raced down the hill, their boots sliding over the hats.

Hollow followed, scanning the horizon for the Princess, the lizard and the rabbit. He had only taken his eyes off them for a second.

Where could they have gone?

Fortunately, Cosentino wasn't running away. He was just standing there next to the fallen hat. If Hollow could catch him, he could make the magician tell him where the others had gone.

Hollow ran closer and closer.

Cosentino still wasn't moving. Spelldust floated through the air around him.

"I've got you!" Hollow snarled, as he tackled the magician—

But Cosentino wasn't there.

It was just an empty cardboard costume.

ABRACADABRA

When Cos threw the hat into the sky—a classic piece of misdirection—he had slipped out of the costume and propped it up, leaning the two sheets of cardboard against one another. He, Snuggles, the Professor and Princess Priscilla had crouched behind the costume. It was a tight squeeze.

Cos could hear Hollow running toward them. "Now what?" he whispered.

"I can disappear," Snuggles said, and she did.

"Me too," the Professor said, and he transformed himself into a top hat, which blended in with the pile under their feet.

"What about us?" Cos asked Priscilla. Cos could hear Hollow and the two soldiers getting closer.

Priscilla was making a shallow hole in the pile of hats. It looked like she was digging a grave.

"I'll hide here, under the hats," she said. "But there won't be room for both of us. Where do you live?"

Priscilla was the King's niece. Was it safe to give her his Nonna's address?

"Quickly!" Priscilla hissed.

"Copperfield Cottage, 8 Burton Lane, Coppertown," Cos said. "But—"

"ABRA-CADABRA!"

And suddenly Cos was back in Nonna's living room.

Nonna **spat** her tea all over the rug. "Goodness me," she said. "Where did you come from?"

"I . . ." Cos turned around, dazed. "What time is it?"

Cos! What happened? Where are Snuggles and the Professor?

"**I don't know.**" Cos sat down on the couch. "Just give me a second."

"Professor," Cos said. "What's going on?"

"Princess Priscilla **saved our lives**," the Professor said. "Hollow and his soldiers are still searching for us in the Land of Lost Hats. As soon as they were far enough away, Princess Priscilla sent us here. She has the power to teleport things over short distances."

"But what about her?" Cos asked. "Where is she?"

"She can't transport herself," Snuggles said. "She said she'd meet us here as soon as Hollow was far enough away for her to escape."

"OK," Cos said. "But we can't just sit here and wait.

we Have an escape To PLaN."

PLAYING WITH FIRE

Cos had laid out several items on the coffee table. He had a new fedora—the Professor had brought it back from the Land of Lost Hats—a magic wand, a silk scarf, and his **spell book**.

"Is this dangerous?" Locki asked.

"Trying a **powerful** new spell while the King's army is already hunting us?" Cos asked. "Nah."

The spell book was highly illegal. The tricks inside were not illusions—they were actual

spells. They could make things fly, or vanish, or transform into other things. They could mend broken objects, or create them out of thin air. They made **miracles possible**.

Cos had discovered the book in his school library, years ago. It was this book which had first made him want to become a magician.

When the King rose to power and banned magic, Cos had taken the book from the library.

He had been just in time—the King's soldiers arrived minutes later and burned the library down.

Reading the instructions in the book, Cos draped a silk handkerchief over the hat. Then he waved the wand and muttered the spell.

"THIS HAT HELPED THE RABBITS VANISH,
BUT TO WARREN THEY'VE BEEN BANISHED.
LET THE MAGIC BE RELEARNED,
SO ITS TENANT CAN RETURN.
ALAKAZAM!"

The magic spelldust raced across the handkerchief and made it disappear.

The magic words faded from the forbidden book, leaving a blank page. This was a single-use spell.

"Well?" Locki said finally. "Did it work?"

"Snuggles?" he said.

Snuggles dived into the hat and scrambled out of sight.

"Hello?" she called. Her voice echoed.

Hello-o-o-o-o-o?

She popped her head back out. "You did it!" she cried. "You opened a portal to Warren!"

Hot diggity!

"But there's no one there," Snuggles continued. "The place is **deserted**."

"They're all in the royal zoo," said a voice from the doorway. "Like I said."

"Priscilla!" the Professor said. "You made it!"

Cos spun around. Priscilla was leaning against the wall. She didn't even look **out of breath**. If it had been hard to outrun Hollow, she didn't show it.

"This may look like an illegal spell book," Cos said nervously, "but it's actually just another one of my illusions. I'm world famous for them."

"Are you really world famous, or just Coppertown-size famous?" she asked, innocently.

Snuggles started choking on a piece of lettuce.

"Because it's funny," Priscilla said, ignoring the rabbit, "I've never heard of you. And if the King or Hollow, or anyone asks, we've never even met. Understood?"

Cos nodded slowly.

"So," Priscilla asked. "Are you ready to **rescue** some rabbits?"

Cos looked around at Nonna, Locki, Snuggles, Ace and the Professor and said,

"we're ready!"

MISSION IMPASSABLE

"Remind me," Cos said. "Why couldn't you just teleport us all into the royal palace?"

"Because the King has cast a **shielding spell**," Priscilla said. "Now keep quiet. We're almost there."

They were inside Priscilla's carriage, driving toward Silver City—a floating city inside a giant mirrored box—which was almost impossible to sneak into.

Locki was hiding in a wooden box near Cos's feet. Professor Camouflage had disguised himself as a velvet pillow. Snuggles had used her powers to disappear. Cos was wearing a costume designed by Nonna, who said the ruffles and the bow tie would make him look like one of the King's birthday guests.

The carriage slowed down as it approached the gates to Silver City. A guard knocked on the window. Priscilla opened it.

Princess! I'll let you through right away.

The guard glanced at Cos, but only briefly. Nonna's disguise had worked.

Priscilla closed the window.

They all heard the gates clank open. The carriage started moving again, now driving on the silver road.

"The guards at the palace will be tougher to fool," Cos said.

Priscilla nodded. "Especially since we need to go through the dock to get to the kitchens and the zoo. Just let me do the talking, OK? Oh no!"

"What?"

Priscilla was staring out the window. "It's Hollow!"

Cos looked. She was right. Hollow was standing on the edge of the moat around the royal palace, peering suspiciously at anyone who walked past.

"He knows you," Priscilla said. "Your disguise won't fool him."

"I can see Hollow's carriage near the drawbridge," Cos said. "It'll be locked, but Locki can get us in. Then maybe we can drive right up to the front gate."

"He'll see us," Priscilla said. "I have a better idea."

Hollow rubbed his hands together to keep them warm. "No sign of trouble at the front gate?" he asked.

The guard next to him raised an orange flag. Up on the distant drawbridge, another guard raised a green flag.

"All clear, sir," the guard with the orange flag said.

A small rowboat appeared under the drawbridge. Hollow **squinted** at it. There appeared to be only one passenger—a young woman wearing a top hat.

She tried to keep rowing, but Hollow stopped her.

"Princess Priscilla," Hollow **sneered**. "Come with me."

Perhaps later. I'm delivering spices to the kitchen for the King's party.

"I wasn't asking," Hollow said. "Where's the magician? And his animals?"

"I'm quite sure I don't know what you're talking about," Priscilla said.

"I saw you at the Land of Lost Hats."

"You did?" Priscilla raised an eyebrow. "Tell me, does the King know you're having his niece followed?"

GET OUT OF THE BOAT!

Am I under arrest? I don't think the King would be pleased . . .

"No," he admitted.

"Then I must deliver these supplies." Priscilla bent to pick up the oars.

"Not so fast." Hollow snapped his fingers.

Guard! Search the boat.

The guard jumped down into the rowboat.

SNAP!

These orders are from the King. All vehicles must be searched. No exceptions.

How dare you!

The search didn't take long. The boat was tiny, and empty—except for a wooden box. It looked big enough to conceal a person.

"What's in the box?" Hollow asked.

"Spice," Priscilla said.

"Spies?!"

"Spice."

"Spies?"

Priscilla sighed. "Just open it."

The guard lifted the lid. A lovely smell filled the air. The box was full of rosemary.

The guard pawed through the fragrant herbs. There was nothing else in the box.

Priscilla raised her eyebrows.

May I go now?

Don't Hold Your Breath

Cos was beneath the water, hugging the underside of the boat. He had been holding his breath now for almost **two minutes**. If Priscilla didn't get the boat out of Hollow's sight within the next **ninety seconds**, he would drown.

Locki was holding on beside him. Padlocks didn't need to breathe.

Snuggles was safely hidden inside Priscilla's top hat. The Professor was disguised as a wooden box.

Seventy seconds.

Cos's lungs were burning. He hoped he hadn't made a terrible mistake.

Fifty seconds.

The oars plunged back into the water and the boat resumed its journey.

Thirty seconds.

Darkness fell above as the rowboat glided into a cave beneath the castle.

KNOCK!
KNOCK!

Priscilla knocked on the floor of the boat, twice. That was the signal.

Cos swam out from under the boat and pushed his way up to the surface. He took a **deep breath**.

"You OK?" Priscilla asked. It would take a few more breaths before Cos could speak. He just nodded.

The underground dock was deserted. Cos and Locki climbed up onto it.

The wooden box transformed into the Professor, who hacked up a bushel of rosemary.

"I could have taken that out first," Priscilla said.

"I assumed you had," the Professor coughed. "Boxes don't have eyes. Or noses."

"OK," Cos said. "Locki and I will go straight to the royal zoo to release the rabbits. It's on the second floor, right?"

Priscilla nodded. "The guards will try to stop the rabbits from leaving."

"The rabbits will go through the hat and into Warren," Cos said.

Priscilla tossed him the fedora. "What about you? How will you get out?"

"Let me worry about that," Cos said. "Professor, you go to the kitchen and stall the chef."

The Professor nodded, and ran along the dock toward the doors.

"The King will be expecting me in the dining hall," Priscilla said.

"Right." Cos held out his hand. "If we don't make it . . . it's been nice knowing you."

Priscilla shook his hand. "You'll make it," she said.

Cos turned to Locki and Snuggles. "Come on," he said.

"we Have RaBBiTS To save."

The chef nodded, satisfied. For the King's birthday dinner, everything had to be perfect. The pans gleamed. The chopping boards were set in neat rows. The ovens hummed happily. And a lizard had just delivered the rosemary. The rosemary was slightly soggy, but the lizard had vanished before the chef had time to yell at him.

Never mind. The herbs would dry in the ovens.

The chef pulled a huge carving knife off his rack of utensils.

"Bring me the first rabbit," he said. "Make sure—"

"A mouse!" **shrieked** his assistant.

The chef **gasped**.

How had it gotten in?

The chef swung the knife.

THUNK!

The mouse leaped off the counter and scampered under the ice box.

"Can't catch me!" it squeaked.

The chef struggled to wrench the knife out of the chopping board. His assistant was still cowering as though he had seen a ghost.

"Stop dithering, you fool!" the chef said. "Help me move the ice box so I can kill it!"

But as he grabbed the ice box with his meaty hands, a cockroach scuttled out from under it. The chef's eyes nearly popped out of his head.

More vermin in his kitchen!

"Yummy, crumbs!" the cockroach giggled.

The chef **stomped** at the cockroach, but it darted out from under his shoes and disappeared into the gap between the pantry and the cupboard.

"YOU KILL THE MOUSE,"

the chef shouted to his assistant.

"I'LL GET THE COCKROACH."

But then he heard a buzzing sound. He looked up. A fly was circling above his head, too fast to grab.

"Buzz, buzz," the fly said. "Where's a good place to drop some maggots?"

The chef was tearing his hair out. If he tried to cook with all these critters in the kitchen, one of them might end up on the King's plate. The chef would lose his job, and perhaps his head.

WWeeeeeeeeeeeeeeee

He chased the fly out of the room and slammed the door. "Get a flashlight," he told his assistant. "We can't bring the rabbits in until we've found the mouse and the cockroach."

★·✳·★·

Cos, Locki and Snuggles were running through the royal zoo, looking for the rabbits. They had passed a grumpy-looking elephant, a lion and a mixture of blue and orange flamingos, but they couldn't see—

"Aha!" Cos said. "Do you smell something?"

"Lettuce," Snuggles breathed.

"Right. This way!"

They ran through a doorway into a room with hundreds of enclosures.

Snuggles' eyes brimmed with tears. The other
rabbits remembered her, after all these years—
and they were so cheerful, even trapped in these
cramped enclosures.

"Locki," Cos said. "Let's get them out."

Locki and Cos
started picking the
locks and opening
the cages.

Locki was much faster
than Cos, but even so, it
would take them a while.
There were hundreds of
locks to get through.

A fly buzzed into the room and transformed into Professor Camouflage.

"The kitchen staff are well and truly distracted," he said. "But we have a big problem."

"What is it?" Cos asked.

Then he heard it. The **yelling** of muffled voices, and the **pounding** of fists on huge wooden doors. **"THE GUARDS KNOW WE'RE iN HERE,"** the Professor said.

"I've locked the main doors to the zoo, but it won't be long before they find a way in."

Cos clenched his fists. His whole plan depended on them getting out undetected. If the guards had already found them, then their escape was over before it even began.

Locki finished unlocking the last cage. Rabbits ran around his feet, stretching their paws and sniffing the floor.

Locki snatched the hat off Cos's head. "Everyone in," he yelled.

The rabbits looked at each other.

"THERE'S NO WAY WE'RE ALL GOING TO FIT IN THERE," a brown rabbit said.

"It's a portal to Warren," Locki said. "We found a spell which—"

"Warren?!" the rabbit screeched, and he knocked Locki over in his desperation to get into the hat. The other rabbits followed. Soon Locki was buried under a stampede of furry creatures, wriggling into the hat two at a time.

Snuggles was last. She looked back at Cos, Locki and the Professor.

I'm gonna miss you guys.

We'll see you again, I promise.

Blinking away a tear, Snuggles scrambled into the hat and disappeared.

More **thumps** echoed from the distant doors.

"Those doors are the only way out," the Professor told Cos. "There's no way we can sneak past the guards."

Then let's give them a show!

RAMPAGE

"What's the holdup?" Hollow yelled. "Get these doors open!"

"They're locked from the other side," one of the guards said.

"I'm not paying you to make excuses!"

"You're not paying me at all," the guard **grumbled**—he was here only because of the King's mind-control spell.

"Get the battering ram!" Hollow ordered.

The guard ran toward the armory.

Hollow **glared** at the entrance to the zoo. He had known that there would be trouble. Spotting the illusionist at the Land of Lost Hats—the day before the King's birthday—had been a bad omen.

Matchman appeared, his wooden hands trembling with excitement.

Hollow grabbed Matchman. "This is your fault. If you'd **killed** the illusionist like I told you to, none of this would have happened."

I burned the building down. How was I supposed to know he would escape?

He's an escape artist, you fool!

Matchman's head started to **glow with rage**. "Don't talk to me that way!"

"Burn this door down," Hollow commanded.

"But this is the King's castle!"

"Do it!"

Flames exploded out of Matchman's mouth. He touched the red tip of his head to the door, and then . . .

SMASH!

The door **exploded** outward, knocking Matchman over and scattering the guards. Hollow leaped out of the way as an elephant thundered through the doorway, **trunk trumpeting triumphantly**.

The flagstones **cracked** beneath the elephant's gigantic feet. On her back were Cos, the Professor, and Locki.

The elephant trotted down the silver stairs, scraping tapestries from the walls. Bits of the door still clung to her tusks.

The guards raced down the stairs, but the elephant was surprisingly fast. Guards fled from their posts as the elephant sprinted through the royal foyer toward the main gates.

"Raise the drawbridge!" Hollow yelled. "Don't let them get away!"

One of the guards turned a huge crank. The drawbridge went up and up, sealing the castle off from the rest of the world.

The elephant stopped and pawed the ground like a frustrated horse, looking down at the moat.

"Got you now," Hollow growled.

The elephant looked back at him. She winked.

Then she jumped.

Hollow had assumed elephants couldn't swim. But he was wrong. The elephant paddled across the moat like a happy dog and easily scaled the riverbank on the other side.

Cos stood up on the elephant's back, and bowed.

Hollow snatched a spear from one of the guards. The blade was **wickedly** sharp.

Hollow hurled the spear like a javelin.

It soared over the river at a deadly speed—

And then it hit Cos.

THE DEAD
MAGICIAN

Cos toppled off the back of the elephant and hit the ground. His hat rolled several feet across the wet dirt and finally stopped.

"Cos!" Locki screamed. He and the Professor leaped off the back of the elephant. The elephant fled, stomping up the King's driveway and disappearing into the winding alleys of Silver City.

Thunder boomed. Rain speckled Cosentino's closed eyelids, and then stopped.

With a **clankety-clank**, the drawbridge came back down. Hollow crossed the moat and strode toward the dead magician. The spear lay beside the body.

As Hollow approached, he saw spelldust leaking out of the fallen hat. He picked it up and reached inside. His arm kept going, deeper and deeper. Just as he had suspected. It had been enchanted. A carriage raced across the drawbridge toward him. Hollow turned to look. He didn't notice a rabbit's paw

reaching out of the hat and into his jacket pocket.

Locki and the Professor had reached the magician's body.

"Cos!" the Professor cried. "Wake up!"

"You're all under arrest," Hollow said. "Guards!"

The magician **groaned**.

Hollow dropped the hat. His eyes widened. "No! It's impossible!"

Somehow Cos was sitting up. Through the hole in his shirt, Hollow could see what looked like . . . a steel plate?

"Guards!" Hollow roared again. "Seize them!"

And then—

WHAM!

Princess Priscilla's carriage knocked him over.

"Snuggles!" Cos hugged his returned friend. "I thought you went home!"

"This is my home now," Snuggles said. "I just had to get some of my old stuff in Warren."

"What stuff?"

"My old copy of *Alice in Wonderland*, my Jefferson Airplane records, a picture of Roger and Jessica—"

"Who are they?" Cos asked.

"My parents."

The carriage zoomed down the King's driveway toward the rest of Silver City. In the rearview mirror, Cos could see Hollow **scrambling** to his feet and running back toward his own carriage. Guards were **dashing** across the drawbridge. It looked like the King's whole army was after them.

"I hate to tell you this," Cos said to Snuggles, "but our new home might be the King's jail. Hollow will be right behind us."

Priscilla spun the wheel, sending the carriage **skidding** around a corner. "I'll try to outrun him," she said. "But his carriage is faster than mine."

"Not without the keys it isn't," Snuggles said. She held up a sparkling key ring.

Cos laughed. "You picked his pocket?!"

"Where would you be without me?" Snuggles said.

Princess Priscilla cleared her throat.

"OK," Snuggles admitted, "the Princess saved our lives too."

"Not yet," Priscilla said. "We still have to get out of Silver City—which, remember, is inside a floating mirrored box several miles above the ground."

"Hollow knows you helped us," Cos said. "Won't he tell the King?"

"Definitely," Priscilla said. "The King won't arrest me, but things could be a bit awkward around the palace. I should 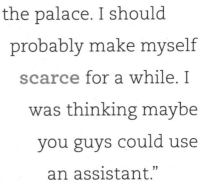 probably make myself **scarce** for a while. I was thinking maybe you guys could use an assistant."

"An assistant?" Cos asked.

"Yes. For the magic show."

Cos raised his eyebrows. "Maybe . . . what are your skills?"

"Well," Priscilla said,

"I CAN SMASH A CARRIAGE THROUGH A GIANT MIRROR AND LAND IT ON THE GROUND BELOW WITHOUT KILLING EVERYONE INSIDE . . . I THINK."

The other passengers looked at each other.

"Does everyone have their seat belts on, by the way?" Priscilla asked.

Cos looked through the windshield. The carriage was rushing toward the mirrored wall of Silver City.

"Everyone hang on to something!" he yelled.

Then the carriage started to fall, **faster and faster.**

"We're going to die!" Locki screamed.

"What's the plan, Priscilla?" Cos yelled.

It looked like the carriage was going to hit the ground right in the middle of Coppertown Square. They'd never survive the impact.

Priscilla pointed one hand at the roof of the carriage and the other at the floor.

"HEY PRESTO!" she shouted.

Spelldust exploded from her hands—

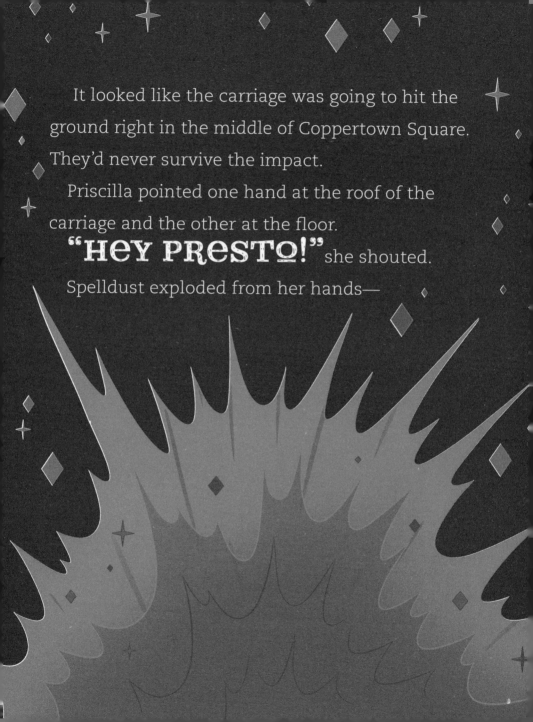

And the carriage started to slow down!

"It's a levitation spell," Priscilla shouted over the roaring wind and the humming magic. "But it's not designed for something this heavy. Brace yourself!"

Cos held on to the dashboard. Snuggles and the Professor clung to their seats. Cos could see people scrambling away from the impact zone. The carriage fell slower and slower until—

It hit the ground with a dull thud. The front of the carriage crumpled and all four wheels fell off, then it rolled onto its side.

"Anyone hurt?" Cos asked.

No one was.

As the **ringing** in Cos's ears faded, he heard another noise from outside. It sounded like **applause**.

"Sounds like you have an audience," Priscilla said. "Do I have a job?"

Cos shook her hand.

"WELCOME ABOARD,"

he said. Then he opened the door—which was now above his head—and climbed out to face the crowd.

You can learn Cos's trick from page 17!

SPONGE SORCERY
MAGIC TRICK INSTRUCTIONS

REQUIRED ITEMS:

4 foam balls

SETUP: Start the trick with two sponge balls in your right pocket and one concealed in the palm of each hand.

METHOD: Ask your volunteer, "Can you hear me OK?" Reach behind your volunteer's ear with your right hand (FIG. 1).

FIG. 1

Quickly move the ball from your palm to your fingertips (**FiG. 2**), and pull your hand back.

FiG. 2

It will look like you have pulled the sponge ball out of the volunteer's ear (**FiG. 3**).

FiG. 3

Say, "That's better. I'll just put that one away." Reach into your right pocket. You're pretending to get rid of the ball in your right hand, but actually you're picking up the other two! Squeeze the three balls tight so they stay hidden (**FiG. 4**).

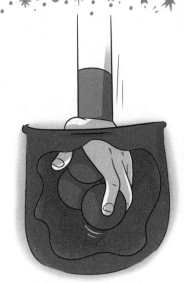

FiG. 4

"Hang on," you say, "there's something in your other ear!" Use the same move to pretend to pull a ball out of your volunteer's ear with your left hand (**FiG. 5**). Now you should have one ball displayed in your left hand and three hidden in your right.

FiG. 5

Say, "OK. Now that you can hear me, it's time to make this ball disappear!" Quickly pass the ball from your left hand to your right, without opening your right hand enough to reveal the three balls already hidden inside (**FiG. 6**). This is the trickiest move. Practice makes perfect!

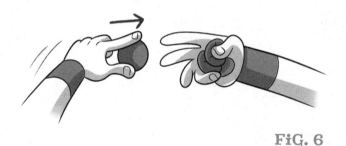

FiG. 6

Make a big show of squeezing your right fist (**FiG. 7**). Pretend this takes great concentration. All the tricky moves are done now, so it's time to perform!

FiG. 7

"Uh-oh," you say. "I think I've done this wrong." Open your fist and let the four balls pop out! (**FiG. 8**).

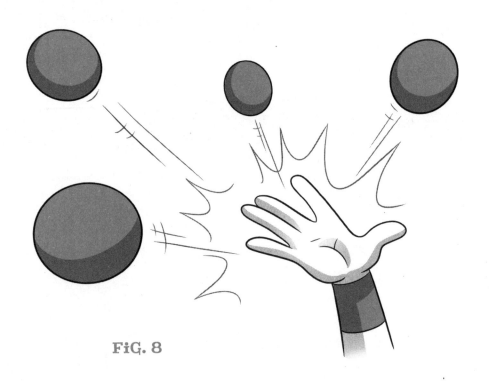

FiG. 8

COSENTINO is now regarded as one of the world's leading magicians and escape artists. He is a multiple winner of the prestigious Merlin Award (the Oscar for international magicians) and is the highest-selling live act in his home country, Australia.

Cosentino's four prime-time TV specials have aired in over 40 countries and he has toured his award-winning live shows to full houses across the world.

Photo credit: Pierre Baroni

JACK HEATH is a bestselling, award-winning Australian author of thrillers and used to be a street magician!

JAMES HART is an Australian children's illustrator who has illustrated many books.